Just Right for Two

nosy crow

For Finlay and Dylan,
with love T.C. xx

For my darling Iris
R.B.

First published in 2013 by Nosy Crow Ltd
The Crow's Nest, 10a Lant Street
London SE1 1QR
www.nosycrow.com

This edition first published in 2013
ISBN 978 0 85763 176 3 (HB)
ISBN 978 0 85763 177 0 (PB)
Nosy Crow and associated logos are trademarks
and/or registered trademarks of Nosy Crow Ltd.

A CIP catalogue record for this book is available from the British Library.

Printed in China

10 9 8 7 6 5 4 3 2 1

Just Right for Two

Tracey Corderoy

Illustrated by

Rosalind Beardshaw

 nosy crow

Dog had a big, blue suitcase.

He took it with him everywhere.

Inside were all his special things . . .

. . . a bumpy little
fir cone,

a pebble, sparkly
and small,

some dancing
leaves,

a really
good stick,

a soft, tickly
feather,

and a big, red shiny
button.

With his special things safely
packed away, Dog watched the moon rise.
"I have everything I need!" he told the stars.
Then he snuggled down on his big, blue suitcase,
which was just the right size for one.

But, next morning, when he woke . . .

. . . someone else was sleeping
on his big, blue suitcase, too!

 "Hey! You can't sleep on here!" cried Dog.

"Oh! Why not?" asked Mouse.

"Because all my special things

are in there . . ." Dog said.

"Can I have a peep inside?" asked Mouse.

"Then I'll go, I *promise!*"

"Just one tiny peep then," nodded Dog.

Mouse peeped inside at Dog's special things.
"I have everything I need in here,"
Dog said.

"Thank you
for showing me, Dog,"
smiled Mouse.

"Now, before I go, how about a game of hide-and-seek?"

Dog thought. "Well, just one tiny game," he said.

So Dog and Mouse
played one tiny game . . .

. . . then a much
bigger one!

Later, when Mouse
went on his way . . .

"Found you!" laughed Dog.
"Oh, playing is quite fun, really!"

. . . the wood felt

suddenly quiet.

To cheer himself up,
Dog opened his suitcase . . .

. . . and gazed at
his special things.
But . . .

"Oh," he sighed.

"Something doesn't feel right . . .

. . . maybe *Mouse*
will know
what it is?"

So Dog set off
to find him.

Luckily, Mouse was not far away.

"Oh, Dog!" cried Mouse. "You look sad.
What's wrong?"

"Well," said Dog. "I thought I had
everything I needed in my suitcase . . .

. . . but now I think I need
something else!
What can it be?"
Dog was so puzzled.
"Don't worry," smiled Mouse,
"whatever it is, we'll find it!"

So Dog searched one way . . .

. . . and Mouse searched the other,
both trying to find the something else
Dog needed.

On and on and on they searched, until . . .

. . . bump!

"It's you!" cried Dog, scooping up his friend.

"You're the **special something** else I need!"

"Me?" wondered Mouse.
"But I'm nothing special."

"You're you!" smiled Dog.
"And that's *very* special."

Later, they shared juicy apples for supper.

"Thank you, Dog," beamed Mouse.

"I've had the best day ever!"

"Me too," nodded Dog,
with a great big,
sticky smile.

From then on, Dog and Mouse
watched the moon rise together.

They sat, side-by-side
on the big, blue suitcase, which
was **actually** just the right size . . .

. . . for two!